Bob the Builder™

Run-Away Roley

by Alison Inches
illustrated by Art Ellis

Ready-to-Read

Simon Spotlight

New York   London   Toronto   Sydney   Singapore

Based upon the television series *Bob the Builder*™
created by HIT Entertainment PLC and Keith Chapman,
with thanks to HOT Animation as seen on Nick Jr.®

SIMON SPOTLIGHT
An imprint of Simon & Schuster Children's Publishing Division
1230 Avenue of the Americas, New York, New York 10020

Manufactured in the United States of America
First Edition
2 4 6 8 10 9 7 5 3 1

Library of Congress Cataloging-in-Publication Data

Inches, Alison.
Run-away Roley / by Alison Inches ; illustrated by Art Ellis.—1st ed.
p. cm—(Bob the builder. Preschool ready-to-read ; 3)
Summary: When Roley the steamroller sleepwalks out of the yard,
Bob the builder rescues him and helps him get back home.
ISBN 0-689-84753-X
[1.Sleepwalking—Fiction. 2. Road rollers—Fiction.] I. Ellis, Art, ills. II. Title.
III. Series

PZ7.I355 Ru 2002
[E]—dc21   2001049351

Honk, shoo! Honk, shoo!

 snored in his .

ROLEY   GARAGE

It had been a long day.

When the sun came up,  was still sleeping.

ROLEY

Then  began to roll

ROLEY

and snore.  was

ROLEY

sleep-rolling!

He rolled toward  .

PILCHARD

"**Meow!**" said  .

PILCHARD

But  kept rolling.

ROLEY

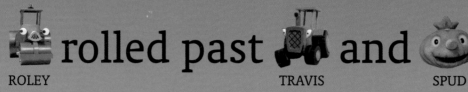 rolled past and .

ROLEY   TRAVIS   SPUD

"Stop!" they shouted.

But 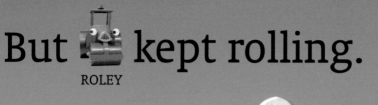 kept rolling.

ROLEY

rolled over .

ROLEY   MAILBOXES

Crash!

And .

GARBAGE CANS

Bang!

ROLEY rolled over

TRAFFIC CONES. **Splat!**

And a . **Bonk!**

LAMPPOST

 even rolled into a .

ROLEY   FENCE

Whack!

Then  rolled straight
toward a big !
ROLEY

HOLE

came running.

BOB

"Look out!"  cried.

BOB

But  kept rolling.

ROLEY

 put over

the ●●● .

BOB   PLANKS

HOLE

Then he put his hands
over his eyes.
"I can't look!" said.

BOB

 rolled over the .

ROLEY   PLANKS

Then he came to a stop.

"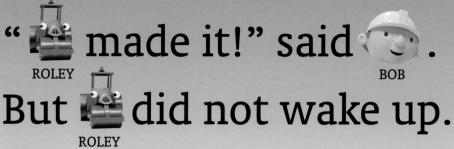 made it!" said .

ROLEY

BOB

But  did not wake up.

ROLEY

"It is getting late. We need  to tow  home," said .

LOFTY

ROLEY

BOB

"Hooray!" said the machines when  got home.

ROLEY

 **ROLEY** opened his eyes. "Hi!" he said. "I had a good rest. Let's rock and roll!"

But everyone was ready for bed.

"Good night, **ROLEY** !"
said the machines.
Then they began
to snore.
Honk, shoo!
Honk, shoo!